STINKER

For Brenda Leach (who first encouraged this
story) and Carla Brown (who found the world's
best dog for my family), with much love
—D.Z.

Dedicated to Alice & Annabel, the biggest
stinkers I know. AJ x
—J.P.

Carolrhoda Books
A division of Lerner Publishing Group, Inc.
241 First Avenue North
Minneapolis, MN 55401 USA

For reading levels and more information, look up this title at
www.lernerbooks.com.

Designed by Emily Harris.
Main body text set in Billy Infant 17/24. Typeface provided by SparkyType.
The illustrations in this book were created with mixed media in a rustic woodshed
in the wilds of Northumberland, next door to a rather stinky dairy farm!

Library of Congress Cataloging-in-Publication Data

Names: Zeltser, David, author. | Patton, Julia illustrator.
Title: Stinker / David Zeltser ; illustrated by Julia Patton.
Description: Minneapolis : Carolrhoda Books, [2017] | Summary: Stinker the dog,
   who often "makes little smells," finds a new home and a new name after a
   lonely, elderly man adopts him.
Identifiers: LCCN 2016008146 (print) | LCCN 2016033570 (ebook) |
   ISBN 9781512417920 (lb : alk. paper) | ISBN 9781512430028 (eb pdf)
Subjects: | CYAC: Dogs—Fiction. | Pet adoption—Fiction. | Odors—Fiction.
Classification: LCC PZ7.Z3985 St 2017 (print) | LCC PZ7.Z3985 (ebook) |
   DDC [E]—dc23

LC record available at https://lccn.loc.gov/2016008146

Manufactured in the United States of America
1-40057-23143-1/18/2017

STINKER

David Zeltser

illustrated by Julia Patton

Carolrhoda Books • Minneapolis

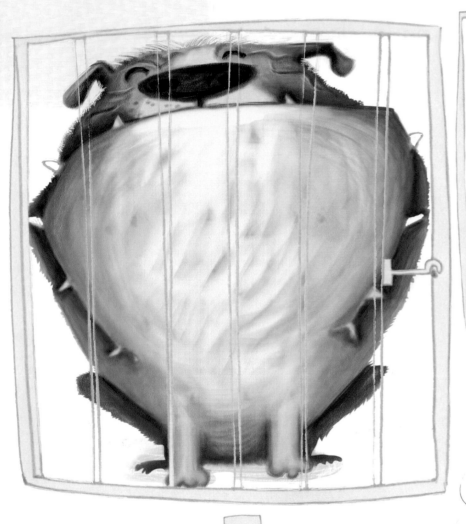

Let me tell you a story. This story
has a **VERY HAPPY** ending.

But, because of **THIS DOG**, it starts out sad. This is Stinker. He has lived most of his life locked up in the pound.

How, you might wonder, did such a sweet-looking doggie get locked up in the first place?

Well . . . when Stinker was a little pup, he ran around nonstop. He barked like crazy.

And he often made little smells.

Stinker's original owner ... **THIS FANCY LADY** ...
did not like seeing him run. Or hearing him bark. And
she *especially* did not like smelling his little smells.

So she sent the puppy off to the pound.

ptt ptt ptt ptt

BUT, since this story has a very happy ending, you have probably guessed that **THIS DELIGHTFUL FAMILY** is going to adopt Stinker.

Guess again.

They thought about it.
And then thought twice.

Pffft

sniff
sniff

So then, surely, **THIS CHEERFUL YOUNG FELLOW** is going to take him home, right?

He got as far as his car, but no farther.

As you can see, this story could go on like this forever.

EXIT →

It could even get depressing.

bark
bark

bark
bark

bark
bark

bark
bark

sigh

But I don't do depressing!

Bus Station

shhh!

THIS IS MR. CURTIS. He is as old as the hills and just as lonely. What he needs most in the world is a friend. And since this story has a very happy ending, you have probably guessed that Mr. Curtis will **SEE** Stinker and welcome him into his home.

Bus Stop

WELCOME to being wrong again.

Mr. Curtis can't see worth a hill of beans. He wouldn't even recognize a hill of beans if he saw one. (Mr. Curtis could *probably* see a mountain of magical glowing beans, but that's another story.)

Wooof!
Wooof!

BUT, since this story has a very happy ending, you have probably guessed that Mr. Curtis will **HEAR** Stinker barking and welcome him into his home.

Hear ye! Wrong ye!

Mr. Curtis cannot hear worth a hoot.
(Mr. Curtis could probably hear
the hoot of a giant owl holding a
megaphone, but that is not the point.)

Now, since this story has a very happy ending,
you have probably guessed that Mr. Curtis will
SMELL Stinker and welcome him into his home.

Finally, at last, you are **RIGHT**!

That is exactly what happens.

toot

Now isn't this a **VERY** happy ending?

ptt
ptt
ptt

Yes, it is.